W9-AHZ-230

©Highsmith® Inc. 1999

Purrfectly Purrfect

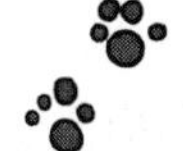

F. CATUS
FOUNDER
THE
ACADEMY

Purrfectly Purrfect

Life at the Acatemy

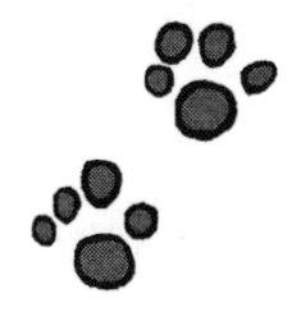

By Patricia Lauber
Illustrated by Betsy Lewin

HarperCollinsPublishers

Purrfectly Purrfect

Printed in the United States of America.

www.harperchildrens.com

Library of Congress Cataloging-in-Publication Data
Lauber, Patricia.
Purrfectly purrfect: life at the Acatemy / by Patricia Lauber; illustrated by Betsy Lewin.
p. cm.
Summary: Describes life at a school for cats, where students learn to be "purrfect."
ISBN 0-688-17299-7 (trade) — ISBN 0-06-029209-1 (library)
[1. Cats—Fiction. 2. Schools—Fiction. 3. Humorous stories.]
I. Title: Perfectly perfect. II. Lewin, Betsy, ill. III. Title.
PZ7.L37024 Pu 2000 [Fic]—dc21 99-50288

1 2 3 4 5 6 7 8 9 10
❖
First Edition

To Willie Thompson, Biggers & Small,
Beemer and MeeToo

—P.L.

To Ajax, Jerky, Bones, Dundee, Slick, and
Chopper

—B.L.

The Acatemy

The Acatemy is a school for cats.

Why, you may wonder, would cats go to school? What might the purrpuss be? After all, as any cat owner knows, cats are born purrfect. But cats are also purrfectionists—they wish to make sure they are *purrfectly* purrfect. And that is why they go to school, if their human owners send them.

The Acatemy, of course, has a catalog. It tells you that the school was founded by Purrfessor F. Catus of the University of Catifornia. It is the purrfessor's belief that "the proper study of cats is cats." The Acatemy, he says, is his "pet project."

The catalog describes the purriculum—Cats in History, Cats in Nature, Cats in Geography, and so on. It tells you that the school color is purrple and . . . But school is about to begin. It is the first day for the new class, many of whom are already looking forward to becoming graducats next month.

A Problem Arises

The head stands at the door, checking off the students, who are lined up to enter. Two students and a kitten present themselves. The head looks at her list. "Bo, Tiffany, and Dudley," she says. "Where is Dudley? And who is this kitten?"

The kitten says, "It's me—Dudley."

That is a problem. Dudley is far too young for The Acatemy. But he's also too young to be sent home alone without Bo and Tiffany. The head decides that Dudley can spend this one day at school.

ACATEMY

Now it is time for assembly. The head welcomes the new class, and everyone joins in singing the school song. The melody just might be "O Christmas Tree, O Christmas Tree," but it's hard to tell:

Acatemy, Acatemy, we sing with deep emotion,
For you do teach us purrfectly
So we may ever purrfect be.
Acatemy, Acatemy, you have our hearts' devotion.

As the students move on to their first class, the head writes a letter for Bo to take home.

THE ACATEMY

September 3

Dear Mrs. Frost:

When The Acatemy accepted Bo, Tiffany, and Dudley, we were not aware that Dudley was only a kitten. The school does not have a kittengarten. Nor can it act as a kitty-sitter. Classes are designed for young cats who are serious students. Please keep Dudley home until he is at least eight months old and ready for The Acatemy.

She also writes to Purrfessor Catus.

THE ACATEMY

September 3

Dear Purrfessor Catus:

You will be pleased to learn that the new term is off to a fine start. We have eleven students. This morning there was also a kitten named Dudley, the younger brother of Bo and Tiffany, but I have written his owner explaining that Dudley is too young for The Acatemy. I am sure that will take care of the problem.

My Summer Vacation

But the next morning there is Dudley, back at school.

Bo explains to the head that wherever they go, Dudley tags along.

Tiffany says They tell him to tag along.

Dudley says he likes to be with Bo and Tiffany.

The head tells Dudley that he must not follow Tiffany and Bo to The Acatemy. She asks Dudley to promise that he will stop.

Dudley promises, rubbing against the head and purring.

The students turn in their homework, essays about their summer vacations.

MY VACATION

by Tiffany

I was sent to camp with my brother Bo. I thought we would roast mousemallows over the campfire and listen to fur-raising stories. But it wasn't like that at all. The very first day we were sent into the woods and marshes to stalk and pounce. My beautiful fur got full of mud and burrs. By the time I cleaned up, the other campers had eaten all the food. So after that I didn't go out. I just hid near the camp.

That's why I didn't win any feathers or become a Kitty Kamper First Klass. But I don't care. My purrsonal dream is to be chosen Miss Americat.

MY VACATION *by Bo*

Tiffany and I went to summer camp. We had a great time creeping through woods and marshes and pouncing on things. I can't wait to go back. Neither can Tiffany. She pretends she didn't like camp, but she was a good little camper who was always on time for meals.

P.S. When we came home, there was a surprise waiting for us--Dudley.

MY VACATION

by Dudley, as typed by Bo

I don't remember a vacation. Maybe I lost it under the refrigerator.

MY VACATION *by Pooh*

While They went on a vacation, I was boarded at the vet's in a nasty little cage with terrible food and a lot of dogs howling all around me. When They brought me home, I accepted food but didn't speak to anyone and spent two days sulking under a bed. After I had punished Them enough, I went back to sitting on Their laps and purring. There is no place like home.

MY VACATION *by Muffin*

We went cruising on a boat. It seemed quite dangerous, so the first few days I hid under a bunk. Then I decided to go on deck. Suddenly the boat tilted, and I fell in the water. Lots of People jumped in after me and put me back in the boat. Water is, like, wet.

MY VACATION *by Tiger*

For my vacation I wanted to visit Santa Claws so I could ask him to bring me two mice, a small rat, and a snake, which would be really cool to have. But Santa Claws is out of season in summer and so I had to go with Them to Grandma Nan's house, where there is nothing to catch except flies.

MY VACATION

by Annie

My vacation was really, you know, weird. We were in this cabin somewhere, and one night when They were asleep, I couldn't find my catnip mouse. Instead, it found me. It was huge and had grown legs. "Now it's my turn!" the mouse said, and it jumped on me, tossed me in the air, and batted me around the room. Finally it got bored and, you know, went to sleep. The next morning it was small again--but it still had legs.

MY VACATION *by Max*

My vacation was, like, WOW! I spent the whole time hanging out. Some of the fellows were quite old, maybe even eighteen months, but they didn't mind us kits. We had a great time talking and things.

MY VACATION *by Rosie*

I would love to tell about my vacation, but it was very private, so I can't.

MY VACATION

by Pumpkin

The highlight of my vacation was the birthday party for Aunt Mary, when I discovered the giblet gravy on top of the refrigerator, a place They didn't think I could reach--ha, ha. Giblet gravy is really super, a delicate blending of chicken juices with just a hint of heart and gizzard and little bites of liver all cut up. If you get a chance, lap it up!

MY VACATION

by Peaches

Some friends and I formed a kitty-sitters club. We had fun planning what we were going to do and how we were going to spend our money. Probably we would have had many adventures if anyone had hired us. But no one did.

MY VACATION *by Tyler*

My vacation was the pits. We visited a farm. First the barn cats chased me. I jumped in a bucket to escape. How was I to know it was full of milk? So then the farmer chased me and I jumped in the next safe place I could see. How was I to know that the hen was about to lay an egg? So then the hens chased me and I hid in some hay and was nearly eaten by a horse!

I ran away and climbed a fence. How was I to know the pigpen was on the other side? It seemed quite dangerous, so I climbed out, ran back to the house, and jumped into the first lap I saw. For some reason, the Person did not seem pleased.

We were supposed to stay for a week, but went home after two days, which suited me purrfectly.

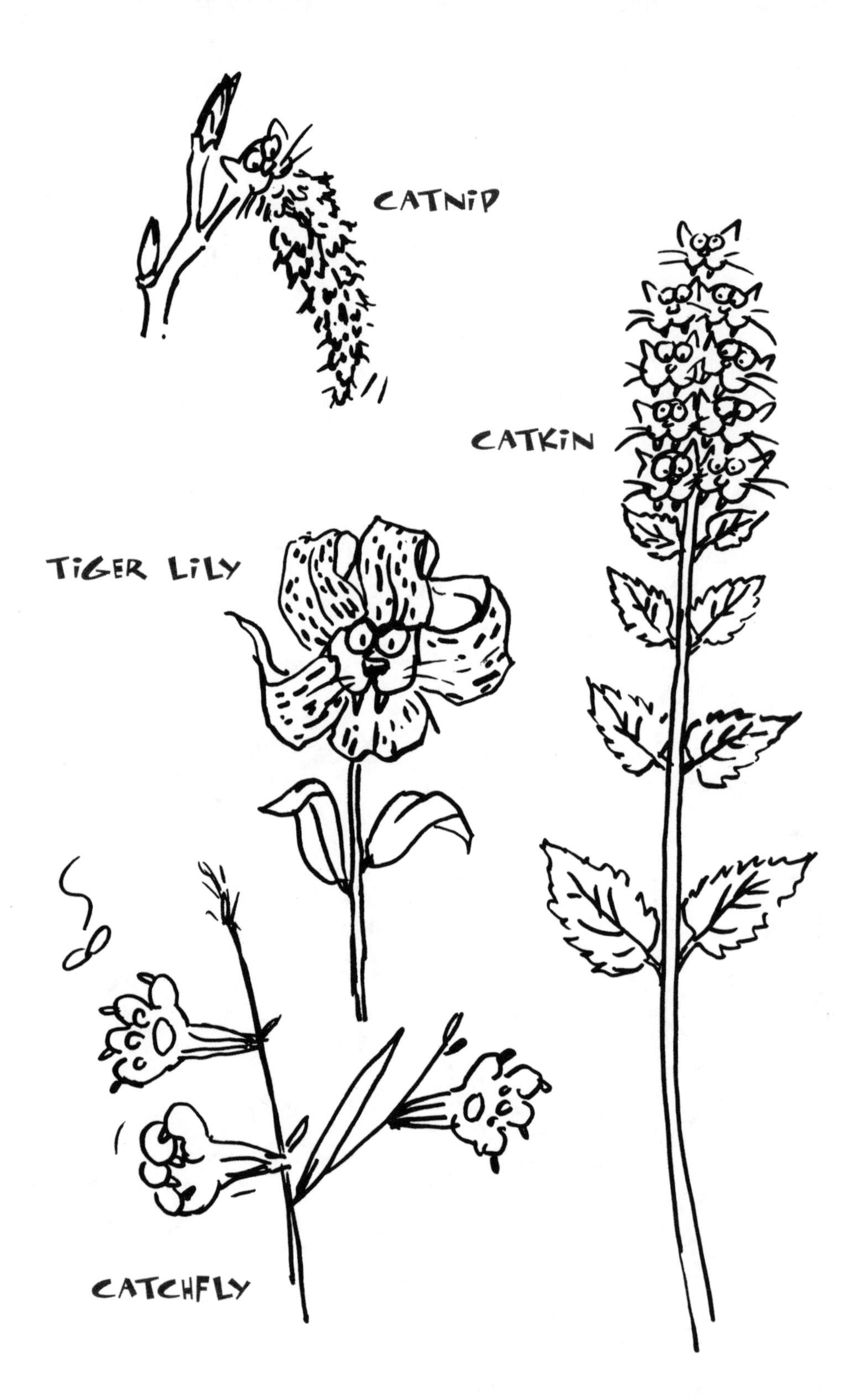
CATNIP
CATKIN
TIGER LILY
CATCHFLY

Cats in Nature

The class has spent several days learning about Cats in Nature. They have looked in books, and they have gone on field trips. Today they are reviewing the many things in nature that are named for cats—or at least sound as if they were. They start with plants, calling out the names as their teacher points to pictures on a chart.

What a lot of plants there are: catnip, cattail, catbrier, catkin, catchfly, dandelion, pussy willow, tiger lily! And dogwood.

Dogwood? Oh, that was Dudley. Bo explains that

their house has a dogwood tree that Dudley likes to climb. The teacher explains to Dudley that dogwood is not named for cats.

Now the class moves on to animals—catbirds, caterpillars, catfish, cattle.

Finally the teacher speaks about cats themselves. As the students know, cats have different colors and markings. Some have long fur, some short. The Manx even has no tail. But all cats have the same shape. They have had the same shape since earliest times. The reason is simple: It is a purrfect shape, especially for being a cat. Dogs, of course, are different.

THE ACATEMY

September 10

Dear Purrfessor Catus:

No, I'm afraid Dudley is still here. As he promised, he no longer tags along after Bo and Tiffany. Now he sets out early and is here before anyone else. He is really a sweet little kitten and is no trouble to anyone, since he sleeps through most of the classes.

Believe me, I am purrfectly aware that he cannot be a student or a graducat and that he must stop attending The Acatemy.

CATSKILL
NEW YORK
CONNECTICAT
KITTY
NORTH CA
NA

THE ACATEMY

September 12

Dear Mrs. Frost:

As I have written you before, Dudley is far too young for The Acatemy. He does not yet have the proper cattitude. Please keep Dudley home!

THE ACATEMY

September 13

Dear Purrfessor Catus:

I beg to differ! I have not permitted myself to be "outwitted by a mere kitten." It is not easy to solve this problem without frightening Dudley and making him a scaredy-cat who will later be afraid of school.

I am sorry to report that Max has left, because his family moved away.

The head really does have a problem. She cannot shut Dudley out, because the purrfessor says that doors and windows must be open at all times so that students can come and go at will. She wishes she could start a kittengarten, but it's too late.

Now they have to work harder. The room grows quiet until Muffin finds Katmandu, the capital of Nepal.

Tiffany discovers Katmai Volcano in Alaska.

Tiger and Max pounce on Catalonia, Spain.

Peaches finds Catasauqua, Pennsylvania.

And Bo sees Kittery, Maine—on the Piscataqua River!

The excitement wakes Dudley, who looks at the map and finds Buffalo, New York. He is told that Buffalo is not a cat name.

A rainy day is a good time for a little geography—for learning the names of places that sound as if they might be named for cats. Each student has a catlas, but most prefer to use the big map on the floor.

The room echoes with squeals as the students quickly pounce on:

The Catskill Mountains of New York
Kitty Hawk, North Carolina
Connecticat
Catalina Island in Purrfessor Catus's home state of Catifornia

Cats in Geography

A rainy day is a good time for a little geography—for learning the names of places that sound as if they might be named for cats. Each student has a catlas, but most prefer to use the big map on the floor.

The room echoes with squeals as the students quickly pounce on:

The Catskill Mountains of New York
Kitty Hawk, North Carolina
Connecticat
Catalina Island in Purrfessor Catus's home state of Catifornia

Now they have to work harder. The room grows quiet until Muffin finds Katmandu, the capital of Nepal.

Tiffany discovers Katmai Volcano in Alaska.

Tiger and Max pounce on Catalonia, Spain.

Peaches finds Catasauqua, Pennsylvania.

And Bo sees Kittery, Maine—on the Piscataqua River!

The excitement wakes Dudley, who looks at the map and finds Buffalo, New York. He is told that Buffalo is not a cat name.

THE A

Sep

Dear Mrs. Frost:

As I have written you before, Dudley is young for The Acatemy. He does not yet ha proper cattitude. Please keep Dudley home!

THE ACATE

Septembe

Dear Purrfessor Catus:

I beg to differ! I have not permitted myself to b "outwitted by a mere kitten." It is not easy to solve this problem without frightening Dudley and making him a scaredy-cat who will later be afraid of school.

I am sorry to report that Max has left, because his family moved away.

The head really does have a problem. She cannot shut Dudley out, because the purrfessor says that doors and windows must be open at all times so that students can come and go at will. She wishes she could start a kittengarten, but it's too late.

The Mewsic Lesson

One day is spent on mewsic. Students raise their voices as they practice catcalls and caterwauling. They rest and listen to a piano piece called "Kitten on the Keys." And they learn that some of the most famous composers have written works called "Magnificat." It is knowledge to treasure.

Reports to Families

The Acatemy does not send out report cards, because all the students are purrfect—not counting Dudley, of course. But after two weeks, the head writes reports to the families.

Tiffany is always purrfectly groomed and on time for lunch.

Bo shows great promise as an athlete. The Acatemy has never had a student who was better at climbing the woodwork.

Dudley MUST BE KEPT HOME.

Annie has a vivid imagination.

Rosie is a cat of few words, but each one is carefully chosen.

Muffin shows care for others and is quick to comfort any student who has been chased under the furniture.

Tyler shows a deep interest in farm life.

Pumpkin has excellent taste. She often visits the kitchen to sample the lunch and make sure it is fit for the others.

Peaches is extremely tidy and cannot bear the sight of loose threads or strings. She has taken it on herself to chew off all the pulls on the window shades.

Tiger is very alert and ready to pounce on anything that moves. He has even managed to knock down two teachers who failed to notice that he was on a windowsill above them.

Pooh may have the makings of a poet. Recently he wrote this little verse:

A trip to the vet's
Is as bad as it gets.
I want to stay home.
That's the end of my poem.

The Lunchroom Mewseum

At noon The Acatemy serves a light lunch. Students are on their best behavior, because the lunchroom also serves as the art mewseum. Its walls have been painted with mewrals of famous figures cats should know.

Catherine the Great of Russia
Richard the Lion-Hearted of England
George Catlin, American artist
Willa Cather, American author
Pleocatra, queen of ancient Egypt
Catilla the Hun, invader of the Roman Empire

Carrie Chapman Catt, American fighter for women's right to vote

And the big favorite, Pounce de León, the famous Spanish explorer who searched for the Fountain of Youth

Spanish Class

Like any good school, The Acatemy likes to build on student interests. Because of the interest in Pounce de León, the head decides to teach a few words of Spanish and a Spanish dance.

She lines up the boys—or mewchachos, as they are called in Spanish class. Each mewchacho chooses a partner from among the mewchachas. While the head plays the catenets, the students dance what seems to be called the catango. At the end each mewchacho bows to his partner and says, "Mewchas gracias."

THE ACATEMY

September 20

Dear Mrs. Frost:

I really cannot make head or tail out of your letter. The Acatemy does not have fountains of any sort, and it most certainly does not encourage students to make fountains out of their water bowls by pouncing on them.

Perhaps you are beginning to understand what I mean when I say that Dudley is much too young for The Acatemy and <u>MUST be kept home!</u>

Sports and Games

Every school day has recess, when the students are free to follow their own purrsuits—to run, jump, climb, chase each other, wrestle, or take catnaps, as they wish. But the school also has sports and games.

The games are simple—catch, cat-and-mouse, cat's cradle, mewsical chairs.

Pussyfooting is practiced.

The chief sport is sailing in The Acatemy's catboat.

Swimming is not a sport, but Dudley goes in the water anyway, saying that he knows how to dog paddle. One of the teachers removes Dudley.

Watching from her window, the head sighs. She wonders if there is some other category she could put Dudley in. He could be the mascat, if cats were team players—but they're not.

Cats and Cars

The students are pleased, but not surprised, to learn that some automobiles have cat names. Cats, after all, are sleek, beautiful, quick, agile, and graceful. And so the names suggest that the cars are too.

Pictures show the cars—a Jaguar, a Mercury Lynx, a Buick Wildcat, a Mercury Cougar, a Mercury Bobcat, a Stutz Bearcat, a Cadillac Catera. There is a picture of a sturdy Sno-Cat, for traveling over snowy land.

Dudley asks why there is no picture of an Eagle. He is told that "eagle" is not a cat name.

There is also a picture of a strange object that no one recognizes. This, the teacher says, is a catalytic converter. There is no need, he adds, to understand exactly what a catalytic converter is. It is enough to know that it is important, so important that no new car may be sold without one.

The students are impressed.

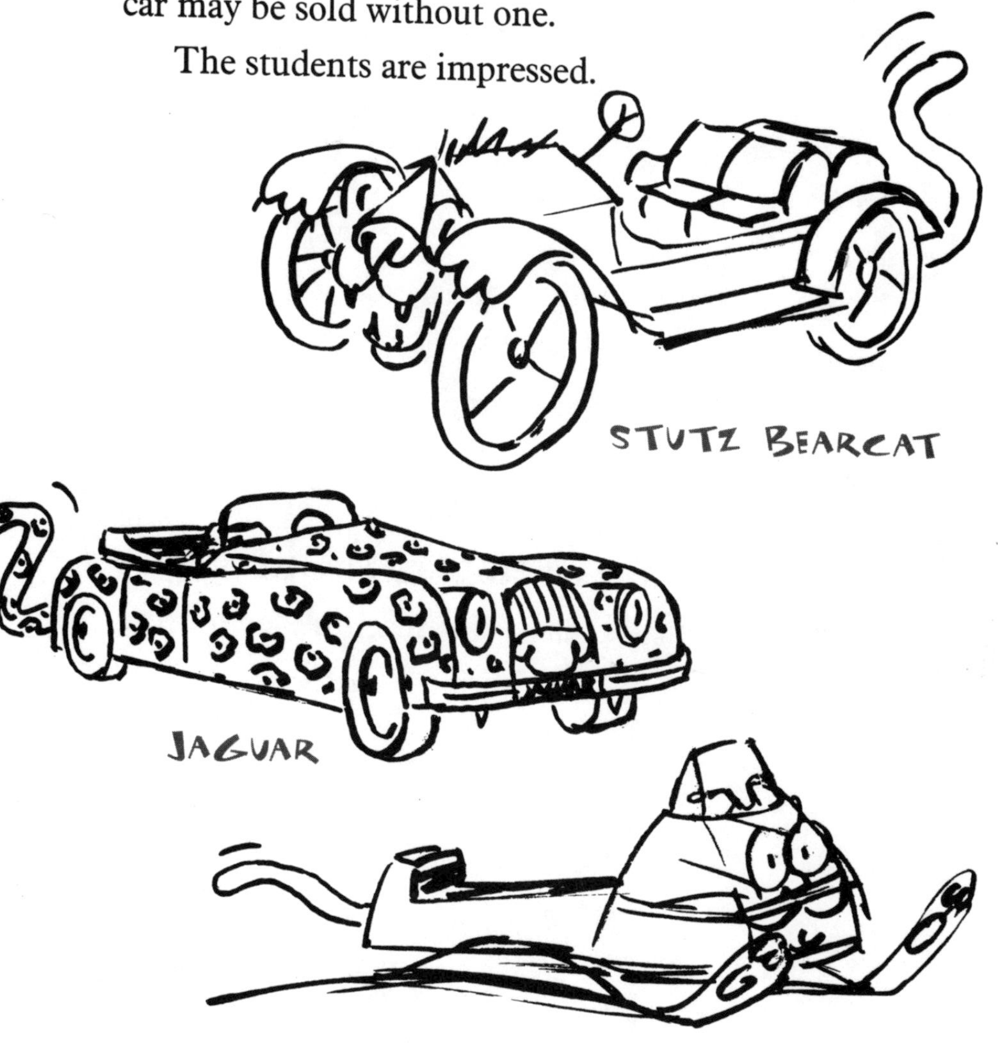

New Cat Words

New words are good to learn, and so there is a course in Vocabulary Building, or, as The Acatemy calls it, Vocatulary Building. The students have learned:

CATASTROPHE: a disaster
CATAPULT: an ancient war machine for hurling rocks; also means to hurl or be hurled

CATARACT: a large downward rush of water
CATACOMB: an underground cemetery, with corridors and holes in the walls
CAT BURGLAR: a burglar who is nearly as stealthy as a cat

Now they are asked to see how many of the words they can use in one or two sentences.

Dudley says he likes the catabrush better than the catacomb and curls up for a nap.

Working together, the other students manage to do even more than they were asked to. They fit all the words into one sentence:

A cat burglar from Katmandu was catapulted into a cataract and buried in a catacomb to the strains of a Magnificat soon after the catastrophe.

Cats in History

As the catalog tells us, The Acatemy prides itself on its course True Facts about Cats in History. The head teaches history herself. What she has to say does not always sound likely, but it is all believed to be true.

Other animals had to be tamed by people. Cats, of course, tamed themselves when the time was right. It happened when ancient peoples learned to raise and store grain. Field mice soon learned that there was no need to scurry around collecting seeds. They could move in and eat the grain people had stored. Then

small wild cats learned that there was no need to waste their time hunting mice. There were lots of mice to be had among the stores of grain. They could move in and catch as many mice as they pleased. That was how people and cats came together. Soon some cats were living with people.

In ancient Egypt, cats were highly valued. The Egyptians believed that their gods and goddesses showed themselves on earth as animals. They had a cat goddess named Bastet and built a huge temple to her. Thousands of cats lived there and were taken care of by priests.

Many other cats lived with families, who loved their cats. When a pet cat died, the whole family shaved off their eyebrows as a sign of mourning. The cat's body was made into a mummy. It was buried in a cat cemetery, with a pot of milk, toys, and whatever else it might need in the next world.

In Egypt, laws said that anyone who hurt a cat would be put to death. And if a house caught fire, the cat had to be rescued first.

By law, no cats could be taken from Egypt. But, of course, many travelers and sailors tried to steal them. And some succeeded.

And that is how cats spread from Egypt into many other parts of the Old World.

Cats reached the New World much later. When colonists left Europe, they naturally took their cats.

During the American Revolution, some cats stayed with their owners to fight for independence. Others moved with their Loyalist owners to Canada.

Later, cats went westward with the pioneers, helping to settle a new country and put down its mice.

Cats worked in homes, shops, factories, and farms, catching mice. They were also soft, warm pets, and that is why they are America's most popular pets today.

The students are bursting with pride. Cries of "Cool!" "Ah, sweet!" "Awesome!" and "Excellent!" echo through the room.

THE ACATEMY

September 27

Dear Mrs. Frost:

Please do not alarm yourself. No matter what Dudley said, The Acatemy does not require the families of its students to shave off their eyebrows.

As I have said before, Dudley is too young for The Acatemy. I must ask you one final time to KEEP DUDLEY HOME! Do NOT send him back to school! This notice is final!

THE ACATEMY

September 27

Dear Purrfessor Catus:

Your letter was most upsetting. I know purrfectly well that every student becomes purrfectly purrfect while at The Acatemy and that The Acatemy has a purrfect graducation record. It is true that I have become rather fond of Dudley, but that is no reason for you to suggest that I get a kitten of my own and stop ruining your pet project. Your project will not be ruined!

What I Want to Be

The end of school is drawing near. It seems like a good time for students to think ahead, to think about the future. They are asked to write essays about what they hope to be when they are grown cats.

WHAT I WANT TO BE

by Tiffany

My dream is still to be chosen Miss Americat. Once I have been crowned, I will appear on TV and be interviewed by Oprah. I will appear in ads for my

favorite foods, which are Kitty Stew, Mealtime, and Chicken and Tuna. Wherever I go, I plan to take Bo and Dudley with me, in case there are mud puddles. They can lie down in the mud, and I will walk across on them, so as not to get mud on my beautiful fur.

WHAT I WANT TO BE

by Muffin

I want to be a mother with many kittens that everyone will gather round and admire. I will take very good care of my kittens and teach them to keep away from water and boats. I plan to have my kittens in the linen closet, where there are lots of nice, soft towels.

WHAT I WANT TO BE

by Dudley, as typed by Bo

I want to be a lapdog.

WHAT I WANT TO BE

by Bo

I am going to enter the Olympics and win contests for rug skidding, jumping on top of refrigerators, and climbing the woodwork. If I had some skates, I could also become a figure skater or maybe a hockey player.

WHAT I WANT TO BE

by Tiger

I am going to become an exterminator and spend all my time hunting and pouncing on mice, snakes, rats, moles, and squirrels. BAM! SPLAT! KAPOW!

WHAT I WANT TO BE

by Annie

I am going to be an astrocat. At night I will get into my box, and it will turn into a spaceship that carries me to the moon and Mars. I will be a fearless space explorer until I get, you know, hungry. Then I'll go home, and it will all seem like a dream except that there will be strange rocks in my box, kinds that no one on Earth has seen before. You know?

What i Want To Be

by Rosie

I would love to tell about my plans, but they are very private, so I can't.

What i Want To Be

by Pooh

I plan to be a housecat who never leaves home. I may also become a writer. We have one in our house, and so I can see what writers do--pacing around, staring out windows, and taking little naps. It is hard work to be a writer, but I am sure I can do it if I try.

WHAT I WANT TO BE

by Pumpkin

I want to be a taster at a big cat-food factory. I will sample the new flavors and suggest adding a little more chicken or beef or perhaps a touch of salmon. You can be sure that all the flavors will have my purrsonal stamp of approval.

WHAT I WANT TO BE

by Peaches

My ambition is to become a teacher, maybe even at The Acatemy. Having almost been a kitten-sitter, I feel I have had lots of experience and could do a good job, unless I become a wizard.

WHAT I WANT TO BE

by Tyler

The first thing I am going to do is to grow into a very BIG cat, maybe the size of a bobcat or even a mountain lion. Then I am going to become an inspector of farms. And when I go to a farm, all the animals and farmers will have to line up and salute while I inspect them. Anybody who doesn't shape up has to jump in the pond and stay there until I say "Come out."

The Head's Problem

With the end of school nearing, the head has a terrible problem—Dudley is still there, and he has failed every course. He cannot be a graducat, but if he is not, The Acatemy's purrfect record of graducation will be spoiled. And if Purrfessor Catus's pet project is ruined, The Acatemy will soon have a new head.

What can she do? The head paces and thinks. There must be an answer, and she will find it. After all, she is purrfectly purrfect, too.

The Eticat Test

Knowing how to behave purrfectly is important, and students have spent many hours talking about eticat. Near the end of school the students take a test. Everyone scores 100—except, of course, Dudley.

1. You are thirsty. Where is the last place you should go for water?

    a) a bowl of flowers

    b) the toilet

    c) whatever you find soaking in the sink

    d) your water bowl

    answer: d

2. You are strolling on the mantel when a valuable ornament hurls itself to the floor and breaks. The best thing to do is:

a) run away from home

b) wash yourself

c) hide

d) lie on the floor with your feet in the air

answer: b

3. You have brought home a big live frog. You should:

a) lay it at your Person's feet and walk away

b) hide it under the rug

c) eat it

d) put it in the toilet

answer: a

4. There are new curtains in the living room. You should:

a) leave them alone

b) climb them to find out if they are sturdy

c) hide behind them

d) purr

answer: b

5. Your Person is too busy in the kitchen to play with you, but lets you out when you ask. You should immediately:

a) insist on being let back in RIGHT NOW

b) go for a walk

c) climb a tree

d) chase snowflakes

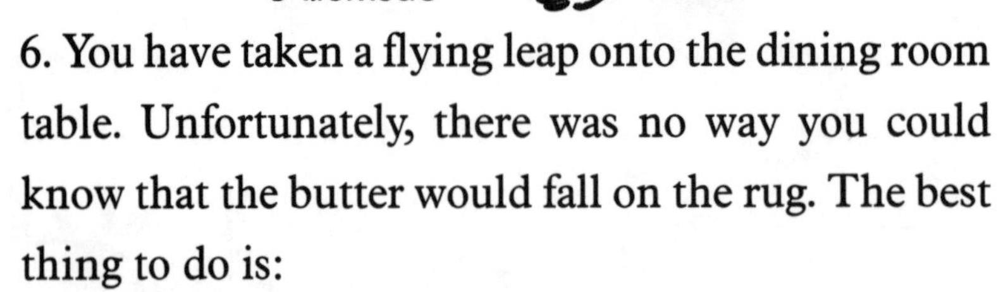

answer: a

6. You have taken a flying leap onto the dining room table. Unfortunately, there was no way you could know that the butter would fall on the rug. The best thing to do is:

a) jump down and be found washing yourself

b) eat the butter before anyone comes

c) hide under a chair

d) cry

answer: a

7. People are playing cards. You should:

a) go to bed

b) play with one of your toys

c) jump up and lie down on the cards so that everyone can admire you

d) bite one of the players on the ankle

answer: c

8. The best place to cough up a fur ball is:

a) outdoors

b) on the kitchen floor

c) on the shag rug in the living room

d) on an old newspaper

answer: c

9. While exploring the kitchen counter, you have discovered a chocolate pie topped with whipped cream. You should:

a) tiptoe daintily through it

b) roll in it

c) leave it alone

d) eat only the cream, because chocolate is bad for cats

answer: d

10. Your sharp ears have picked up a sound that may mean someone is trying to break into your house. The best thing for you to do is:

a) hide under the nearest bed
b) yowl loudly
c) go on with what you were doing
d) see if there's any food left in your bowl

answer: a

11. The cat carrier has been brought out, hinting of a trip to the vet's. You should:

a) pretend to be sleeping
b) cry
c) get under the sofa and cling to the bottom with your claws
d) be a good sport and go without a struggle

answer: c

12. A goldfish bowl has appeared in the living room. You should view it as:

a) a no-no
b) a nice supply of fresh fish, meant for you
c) something the whole family can share
d) something that will break if tipped over

answer: b

13. You are burning off energy by running as fast as you can over the furniture and through the house. You should be careful not to:

a) knock over the lamps

b) scratch the tabletops

c) frighten the guests

d) overtire yourself

answer: d

14. You have been caught using the sofa instead of the scratching post. The best thing to do is:

a) hiss loudly at the scratching post

b) make yourself very small and creep away

c) wash

d) attack the rug

answer: c

15. The most important social rule you can learn is:

a) never raise your voice

b) always eat what is put in your bowl

c) when in doubt, wash

d) keep off the furniture

answer: c

Graducation at Last!

And now the big moment has arrived: Graducation! The ceremony is held outdoors, so that families can attend. Later there will be a tasty lunch catered by a delicatessen, of course. The excited students gather for the school song. Then one by one they are called forward to receive diplomas showing they have proved themselves purrfectly purrfect.

The Acatemy never gives prizes, because no graducat is better than the others—they are all purrfect, each cat in its own way. But something strange is happening. The head, looking like a cat

ACATEMY

who has just swallowed the canary, is announcing a special award. And the winner is—Dudley.

Dudley?

The head is explaining. Being only a kitten, Dudley failed every course, and so his final grade is 0. Not 30 or 12 or even 2, but 0. It is a purrfect 0, a purrfectly purrfect 0, and the first in The Acatemy's history.

Everyone is clapping and cheering for Dudley. Like the cat he will become, he is purrfectly purrfect in his own way.

What Readers Are Saying about This Book

Even though it's about cats, I have to give this book my highest rating: ⋆Woof!⋆ ⋆Woof!⋆ ⋆Woof!⋆

—Morgan, *The Dogville Daily*

Mouthwatering!

—*The Piranha Post*

Outstanding for its semiotic symbolism and nonpragmatic elucidation of the trajectory of deconstruction. A seminal work, deftly configured to appeal to all ailurophiles. Buy it!

—Purrfessor F. Catus
University of California

As appealing as a whiff of catnip! Every cat should have a copy.

—Kitty Cat, *Cat's Life*

Bats are, of course, fascinating. But who would have guessed that they attend a school called The Abatemy? I look forward to reading this book as soon as I have time.

—M. Volans, *The Batty Beacon*

Although this book claims to cover things every cat should know, it has nothing—absolutely nothing—to say about the importance of getting one's shots, having one's teeth cleaned, or eating a proper diet. A parent is told to keep her kitten home but is at no time instructed to change the kitty litter daily. No serious-minded librarian will wish to expose young readers to a book so lacking in tips on health and hygiene. Nor will schools appreciate a book that makes a hero out of a cat who fails every course. Highly unrecommended.

—Dr. I. M. Notamused
Literate Libraries

Our Person worked very hard on this book, and I don't care what Dr. Notamused says. What does he know? It's a great book! I love it.
P.S. I hate vets anyway.

—Beemer
A cat

Me too.

—MeeToo
A cat

This is the best book I have ever read. Until last week I had not read many books.

—Johnny, Grade 4, P.S. 421

Another cat book! I love them, and I can't stop myself from buying them, even though I'm running out of shelf space. This one is most amewsing, if I may have my little joke. Highly recommended for both large and small collections.

—I. M. Helpless
Village Library

I thought the book was a real hoot.

—Olive Owlet
Night owl

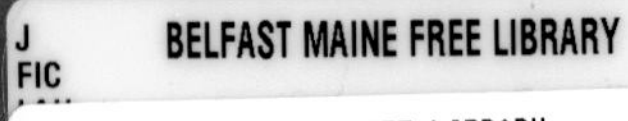